ELISE PRIMAVERA

plantpet

G. P. Putnam's Sons

Bertie lived alone and liked it that way.
His junkyard was high on a hill.

One day when he was out looking at his junk,
he found a tiny plant in a cage.
TURN THIS CAGE DAILY the instructions read.
"I never had a plant before," Bertie said.
He took it home.

Bertie turned the cage every day.
Every day the plant grew and changed.

In fact it changed so much that when Bertie opened the cage
to give it more room, it walked out all on its own.
"What are you anyway!"  Bertie cried. "A plant or a pet?"
But it just kept on going out the door and into the garden.

It seemed to like to dig. Bertie knelt down to help.
"You need a name," Bertie said. "I'll call you Plantpet."

Side by side in the long-neglected garden, Bertie and
Plantpet weeded and watered, planted and pruned.

Every day they worked together in the warm sun.
The garden grew and changed.

"I never had a pet before," Bertie said. "Good boy,
good boy."

Finally the garden bloomed. It was absolutely beautiful
and Bertie was proud of it. "Suits me just fine," he said.
But Plantpet kept on digging.

"No! No!" Bertie cried. "Bad boy! Bad boy! No dig hole! Hole bad!" Bertie shouted.

But Plantpet kept on digging a hole—a Big hole...

...until finally Bertie gave up and took it to the farthest corner of the garden. "Stay," he said.

Now every day Bertie worked in his garden alone.
But it just wasn't the same. Something was missing.
He raced back to the farthest corner of the garden.

"My poor little friend," he cried. Bertie gently picked up Plantpet and they went home.

Bertie dug a hole. He placed his friend inside it.
"Here's some warm dirt to cover your toes," Bertie said.
"And here's a drink of water."

Plantpet grew and changed.
Sometimes Bertie worked in the garden and his friend watched.

And sometimes they rested together,
which suited them both just fine.

Reprinted by arrangement with G.P. Putnam's Sons, a division of
The Putnam & Grosset Group
Printed in the U.S.A.
G. P. Putnam's Sons, a division of The Putnam & Grosset Group,
200 Madison Avenue, New York, NY 10016.
G. P. Putnam's Sons, Reg. U.S. Pat. & Tm. Off.
Published simultaneously in Canada.
Book designed by Elise Primavera and Nanette Stevenson.
Text set in Trump Medieval.

Library of Congress Cataloging-in-Publication Data
Primavera, Elise.   Plantpet / Elise Primavera.   p. cm.
Summary: In his junkyard Bertie discovers a life form fond of gardening,
but he nearly loses his new pet by not understanding it needs.
[1. Plants—Fiction. 2. Pets—Fiction. 3. Gardening—Fiction.]
I. Title. II. Title: Plant pet.
PZ7.P93535P1   1994   [E]—dc20   93-36526   CIP   AC
ISBN 0-399-22627-3

10  9  8  7  6  5  4  3  2  1

First Impression